Nate the Great
SAN FRANCISCO DETECTIVE

Nate the Great
SAN FRANCISCO
DETECTIVE

by Marjorie Weinman Sharmat
and Mitchell Sharmat

illustrated by Martha Weston
in the style of Marc Simont

A Yearling Book

Published by
Yearling
an imprint of
Random House
Children's Books
a division of Random House, Inc.
New York

SPECIAL GUEST APPEARANCES BY

Olivia Sharp, Willie the Chauffeur, and Duncan

from the Olivia Sharp, Agent for Secrets series
by Marjorie Weinman Sharmat and Mitchell Sharmat

Visit us on the Web! www.randomhouse.com/kids

Educators and librarians, for a variety of teaching tools, visit us at www.randomhouse.com/teachers

ISBN-13: 978-0-440-41821-4
ISBN-10: 0-440-41821-6

Reprinted by arrangement with Delacorte Press
Printed in the United States of America
One Previous Edition
New Yearling Edition May 2005
18 17 16
UPR

For our granddaughter
Madeline Lucille Sharmat
with much love

—M.W.S.

—M.S.

For the Shopoffs,
my San Francisco family

—M.W.

CHAPTER ONE
MR. GREAT

My name is Nate the Great.
I am a detective.
My dog, Sludge, is a detective too.
This morning Sludge and I were
at the airport in San Francisco.
We were supposed to meet
another detective there
at ten o'clock.
My cousin, Olivia Sharp.
Olivia always wears a boa
made of feathers.
This makes her easy to find.
Anywhere.
But all we saw were strangers.
And many people with signs.

All at once, I, Nate the Great,
saw a sign that said
NATE THE GREAT
in big letters.
A man in uniform was holding it.
He came up to us.
"Mr. Great and Sludge?" he said.
"I'm Willie. Miss Olivia's chauffeur.
She's out on her eight o'clock case.
It's running late.
She hasn't even started
her nine o'clock."
Willie picked up my suitcase.

"Your limo is over there," he said.
"My limo?"
"Yes. Miss Olivia always
travels in a limo.
But today she saved it for you."
I, Nate the Great, had never
been in a limo.
Sludge had never been in a limo.
It was long and shiny.
We got inside.
Willie got in the front seat.
And we were off.

CHAPTER TWO
CALLING
NATE THE GREAT

We drove up and down many hills.
"Is everything all right
back there, Mr. Great?" Willie asked.
I looked at Sludge.
He wagged his tail.
"Fine," I said.

"But can you tell me about the case
that's making Olivia late?"
"Her friend Duncan
lost a joke book," Willie said.
"Miss Olivia is looking for it."
Willie drove us to Olivia's house
and let us in.
A telephone was ringing.
And ringing.
This was a phone that
needed to be answered.

"Nate the Great for Olivia Sharp,"
I said.
"Hello, Nate."
It was Annie, from back home.
"We all miss you," she said.
"And Fang has something to tell you."
I heard heavy breathing.
I knew that Annie's dog, Fang,
was on the line.
I was happy to be many miles away
from his teeth.

I waited.

Fang had nothing else to say.

Then I heard a strange voice.

It belonged to Rosamond.

"My turn. Bring back California fish

for my cats. Lots of fish.

All the fish you can carry.

Over and out."

"I thank all of you

for the call," I said.

Then I heard another voice.

"Wait! It's me, Claude.

I lost something."

Claude was always losing something.

"I lost an itsy bitsy seashell

two years ago

on the Golden Gate Bridge.

Find it!"

Claude hung up.

CHAPTER THREE

THE END
OF THE WORLD

The telephone rang again.
"Nate the Great for Olivia Sharp,"
I said.
"Hello. This is Duncan.
It's eleven o'clock
and the world is coming to an end."
I, Nate the Great, hoped that
this Duncan person did not have
his information straight.

"I need Olivia," Duncan said.

"Olivia is out," I said.

Duncan moaned.

"Then the world
is really coming to an end."

"Could you be more specific?" I asked.

"Well," said Duncan,
"I lost my joke book.
I have to tell a joke
to a friend at two o'clock
and I forget how it ends."
"Olivia is on your case," I said.
"Yes, I'm her case number twenty-two,"
Duncan said.
"But she is also working on cases number
eighteen and number
twenty-one at the same time.
She'll never solve mine
by two o'clock."
I, Nate the Great, had never
heard such a sad voice.
"Very well," I said. "I will also
take your case."
I hung up.
Then I called my mother.

The answering machine came on.
I said,

"Dear Mother,
Sludge and I are on
a California case.
But it has something
to do with
the entire world.
Or the end of it.
Something like that.
I will be back.
Love,
Nate the Great."

CHAPTER FOUR
JOKE STEW

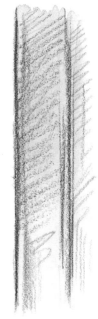

Willie drove Sludge and me
to Duncan's house.

"I will wait in the limo," Willie said.

I knocked on Duncan's door.

He answered it.

Duncan looked even sadder
than he sounded.

His hair was hanging limp,
his socks were drooping,
and his jeans were slipping.
Sludge and I walked inside.
"I am Nate the Great," I said.
"And this is my assistant, Sludge.
Tell us about your joke book."
"Well, I was in Booksie's Bookstore
yesterday," Duncan said.
"I saw this small book
called *Joke Stew*.
It was the only copy there.
I bought it.
I left the bookstore
with the book in a Booksie's bag."
"Then what did you do?"
"I went to lots of other stores
and bought things.
Then I went to Perry's Pancake House."

"A *pancake* house? Good thinking."
"Yes, Perry's Pancake House has
this big, big menu with five pages
of different kinds of pancakes.
I started to read the menu.
The waiter came by.
I ordered mushyberry pancakes.
The waiter left.
I kept reading the menu.
Then I took out my joke book
to find the perfect joke
to tell today.
I found it."

"Then what happened?"

"The waiter brought the pancakes."

"Did you put the joke book
back in its bag?"

"I don't remember," Duncan said.

"Because something bad happened."

"What happened?" I asked.

Duncan looked down at his feet.

"I can't tell you."

"What *can* you tell me?"

"The world is coming to an end."

I, Nate the Great, wished this case
were coming to an end.
I said, "So the last place
you saw your joke book
was in the pancake house?"
"Yes."
"It might still be there," I said.
I, Nate the Great,
was sure of one thing.
Pancakes were still there.
Five pages of pancakes to choose from!
"I will be back," I said.

CHAPTER FIVE

STICKY, ICKY MESS

Willie drove Sludge and me to
Perry's Pancake House.

"Sniff around outside, Sludge," I said.

"Look for the joke book."

"I'll help Sludge," Willie said.

I went inside the pancake house.

It looked good, it smelled good.

I walked up to a waiter.

"I am looking for a small joke book titled *Joke Stew*," I said.

The waiter looked mad.

"A girl was just here looking for it," he said.

"She was wrapped in feathers. Said she was a detective.

She put up LOST JOKE BOOK signs everywhere.

Here. There. Up and down the street.

But we have no joke book.

I know who lost it.

Yesterday this boy came in.

I served him mushyberry pancakes.

He knocked the syrup bottle over everything.

The pancakes, the menu, the table. Ugh!

I scooped up all the sticky stuff
and dumped it in a bag.
I handed the bag to him.
I told him that somewhere out there
a hungry family of ants or flies
would love this sticky, icky mess."
The waiter was getting madder.
I, Nate the Great, knew that I
had to leave the pancake house
without eating.
I did not want to do that.
But I went outside.
Sludge and Willie were standing there.
"We didn't find the joke book," Willie said.

"We looked in front.
Then Sludge went out back.
He found garbage cans.
He looked in them.
Isn't that the wrong place to look
for a joke book?"

"Well, a good detective knows
that sometimes the wrong place
is the right place," I said.
"Smart dog," Willie said.
Willie, Sludge, and I got into the limo.

CHAPTER SIX
THE GOLDEN GATE CLUE

I liked this limo.
It was a good place to think
and to drive around
to see San Francisco.
I, Nate the Great, was thinking.
I was not having any luck
with Duncan's case.
I had not found his joke book.
I had not found Claude's seashell either.
Perhaps that was because
I had not looked for it.
"To the Golden Gate Bridge,
please," I said to Willie.
"A fine bridge, Mr. Great," Willie said.

When we got there,
Sludge and I peered out the window.
The Golden Gate Bridge
was very, very big.

Claude's seashell was
very, very small.
This was not going to help Claude.
But suddenly I, Nate the Great,
knew that it might help Duncan!
"I have a Golden Gate clue,"
I said to Willie.
"Onward to Duncan's house!"

CHAPTER SEVEN

FROZEN PANCAKES!

Duncan was waiting for us.

"I know all about the spilled syrup," I said. "What did you do with the bag the waiter gave you?"

"I put it in the freezer," Duncan said. "I like frozen pancakes."

"Did you open the bag first?"

"No, it was too icky and sticky."

I put my hand on Duncan's shoulder.
"I, Nate the Great, know
where your joke book is.
It is in your freezer!"
"Oh, cool!" Duncan said.
Was that a joke?
Never mind.
"I, Nate the Great, say
you were reading the menu.
But you were also reading your joke book.
The menu was big. The book was small.
So the book must have slid
or fallen into the pages of the menu.
Before or while the syrup spilled.
The waiter scooped everything up fast
and put it all in a take-out bag."
"You are a good detective," Duncan said.
"Even if you don't put up signs."

"No problem," I said.
"Olivia has her way. I have mine."
I opened the freezer.
I saw the bag.
I took it out.
I opened it.
It was full of cold, crusty, icky things.
Pancakes, napkins, the top
from a syrup container,
a little tub of butter,
a huge menu . . .

but no joke book!

"The joke book isn't here," I said.
"The world is definitely
coming to an end, correct?"
Duncan looked down at his feet.
"Correct," he said. "I need my book
at two o'clock. And it's after twelve now."
"Do not lose hope," I said.
"That is the worst thing to lose."
I sat down.
"I, Nate the Great, need pancakes.
Sludge needs a bone.

They help us think."
"Have a frozen pancake," Duncan said.
"Thaw it," I said.
"I don't thaw," Duncan said.
"Very well," I said.
"A frozen pancake is
better than no pancake at all.
But give Sludge a nice bone."

CHAPTER EIGHT
LOST IN THE BIG CITY

I ate a frozen mushyberry pancake.
It did not help me think.
Except about my cold teeth.
"What happened after you left
the pancake house?" I asked.

"Well, I had lots of bags.
I dropped them outside
the pancake house.
Then I picked them up
and brought them home.
I put the pancake bag in the freezer
and the other bags over there
in that corner.
But the Booksie's bag isn't there."
"Hmmm," I said.
I went over to the corner
and looked inside all the bags.
No book.
"Both the book *and* the Booksie's bag
are missing," I said.
"I, Nate the Great, say
that we should go
to Booksie's Bookstore.

I think you dropped your book
in its bag when you were
in front of the pancake house.
It wasn't there today.
Perhaps somebody found it
and took it back to the store."
Duncan kept looking at his feet.
"Somebody could have found it
and taken it home," he said.
"Or taken it on a trip.
Or mailed it. Or kicked it.
Anything! This is a big city.
My joke book could be anywhere!"
"You are right," I said.
"I *am?*"
"Yes. This is a big-city case.
Your book *could* be anywhere.
But we don't have enough time
to look everywhere.

So I, Nate the Great,
have to *choose* where to look.
And because the book was probably in
the Booksie's bag when you lost it,
I choose Booksie's Bookstore."
"Oh," Duncan said. "There
is more to this detective
business than I thought."

CHAPTER NINE
WHAT'S WRONG IS RIGHT

Willie drove Duncan, Sludge, and me
to Booksie's Bookstore.

He waited outside with Sludge.

Duncan and I went inside.

"Are books returned here?"

I asked a lady behind the counter.

"Yes."

"Was a joke book returned today
or yesterday?"

"You're the second person to ask,"
the lady said. "A girl with a feather boa
and a bunch of signs
was just asking the same question.
I told her a mystery book
had been returned.
And a children's book,
a cookbook, and a science book.
But no joke book."

"What happens when a book
is brought back?" I asked.
"We put it on the shelf again," she said.
Duncan and I walked away.
"Show me the joke book department,"
I said.
"Why? It won't be there," Duncan said.
"We can't be positive," I said.

Duncan led the way.
"Here," Duncan said. "This is
the exact place I found the book."
I looked around.
I looked hard.
The book *wasn't* there.
"You did not choose the right
place in the city to look," Duncan said.

I, Nate the Great, already knew that.
I saw Sludge peering
through the front window.
Sludge had not been much help
on this case.
Or had he?
He had looked in the wrong place
for the joke book.
But he knew that
sometimes the wrong place
is the right place.
The wrong place!
"Follow me," I said to Duncan.
I rushed up and down aisles.
At last I came to the place
I was looking for.
The wrong place.
I waved to Sludge.
He wagged his tail.

Then I looked up and down
and across shelves.
And there it was!
Duncan's joke book.
Joke Stew!!!
I took it down
and handed it to Duncan.
"My book! My book!" he said.
"But this is the cookbook section.
Why is my book *here?*"

"I, Nate the Great,
say that the lady told us
a cookbook had been returned.
Whoever put your book
back on the shelf
thought it was a cookbook.
With a name like *Joke Stew*,
it could be."
Duncan smiled. He *smiled*.
I knew the world was safe for now.

CHAPTER TEN
A FEATHERY HUG

Duncan skipped off.

Suddenly I heard a voice.

"You solved my case number twenty-two!"

A bunch of feathers hugged me.

It was Olivia. In person.

"I owe you one," she said.

"Let me know if I can ever

solve a case for you. Any case.

Big, small, easy, hard."

"I think I have something
for you right now," I said.
"It's big and it's small
and possibly it's hopeless.
Willie can take us to it."
I, Nate the Great,
enjoyed the ride
back to the Golden Gate Bridge.

~Extra~
Fun Activities!

What's Inside

NATE'S NOTES:
The Golden Gate Bridge

The Golden Gate Bridge sits in a huge park. It's one of the world's largest city parks. The park has twenty-four miles of beach. It also contains redwood forests, sea cliffs, and mudflats. Many rare animals live in the park. Plants too! Every year, about 16 million people go there to play.

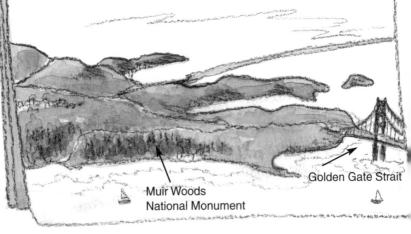

Muir Woods
National Monument

Golden Gate Strait

The Golden Gate Bridge is orange. So why don't we call it the Orange Gate Bridge? Because the bridge is named after the Golden Gate Strait. A strait is a narrow waterway. The Golden Gate Strait flows under the bridge. It connects the Pacific Ocean with San Francisco Bay.

A group of about fifty workers keeps the bridge in good shape. The workers climb the bridge—even in the wind and fog. Sometimes they put in new rivets. Rivets are like big nails. They hold the bridge's steel towers together. Sometimes the workers paint the towers and cables. Paint protects the bridge from the salty sea air.

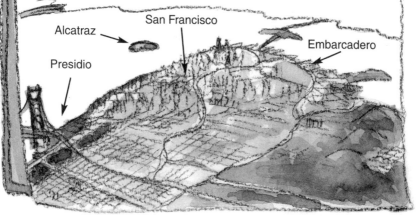

Alcatraz

San Francisco

Presidio

Embarcadero

3

The Golden Gate Bridge took more than four years to build. Eleven men died building it. Nineteen more fell while putting the towers together. They landed in a safety net. The net saved their lives!

The bridge opened to traffic on May 28, 1937. High winds have closed the bridge three times. Earthquakes have shaken it. But it's still standing strong.

The **Golden Gate Bridge** under construction

As of May 2004, a total of 1,775,780,649 vehicles had crossed the bridge.

The Parts of a Suspension Bridge

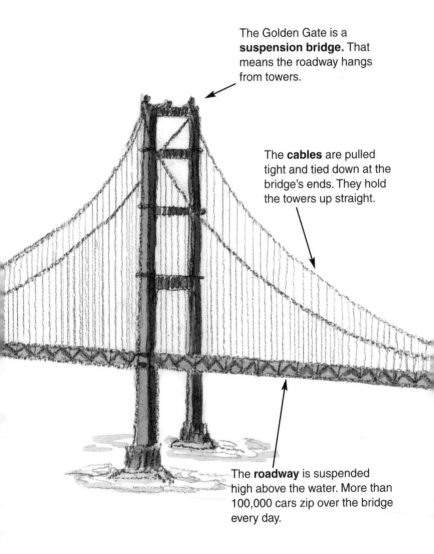

The Golden Gate is a **suspension bridge.** That means the roadway hangs from towers.

The **cables** are pulled tight and tied down at the bridge's ends. They hold the towers up straight.

The **roadway** is suspended high above the water. More than 100,000 cars zip over the bridge every day.

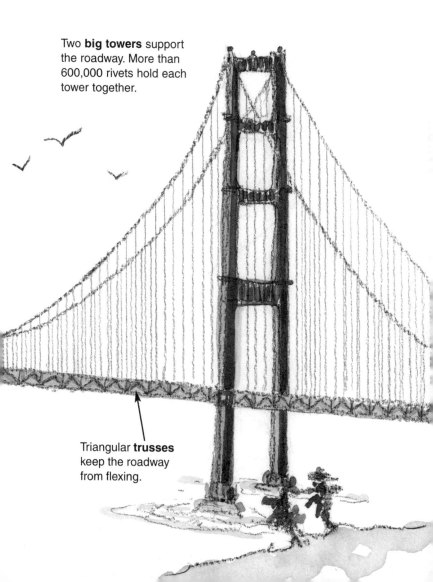

Two **big towers** support the roadway. More than 600,000 rivets hold each tower together.

Triangular **trusses** keep the roadway from flexing.

NATE'S NOTES:
Things Lost and Found

Nate didn't find Claude's shell. Maybe finding a shell on a big bridge is too hard. Maybe not. Check out these other amazing things people have found:

POMPEII

In 1594, well diggers in southwest Italy found part of a buried temple. Over the next 300 years, people slowly unearthed an entire city! The city was called Pompeii. A nearby volcano called Vesuvius had erupted in AD 79. Lava and ash buried the city. It stayed hidden for almost 1,500 years.

As diggers went to work, they found people "frozen" at the moment of death. They found tables set for dinner. They even dug up whole eggs!

THE *TITANIC*

In 1912, the largest ship ever built set sail from England. It was headed to New York. Four days later, the ship hit an iceberg. The ship broke in two. Then it sank. About 1,500 people drowned. The *Titanic* stayed lost for seventy-three years. Scientists using deep-sea submarines with cameras found the ship off the coast of Canada. The *Titanic* rests more than two miles down, on the bottom of the sea.

KING TUT'S TOMB

An Englishman named Howard Carter dug up King Tutankhamen's tomb in 1922. King Tut had ruled Egypt more than 3,000 years earlier! An amazing treasure was inside. Carter found a gold mask, a throne, jewels, and more. He even found the king's mummy! It lay inside three nesting tombs. The smallest tomb was solid gold.

ICE MUMMY

In 1991, mountain climbers found a mummy near the border between Italy and Austria. It was inside a glacier. The ice had kept the body intact. The mummy wore a grass cape. He carried bows and arrows. His shoes were stuffed with grass to keep his toes warm. Scientists say the mummy died around 3350 BC. He'd been hidden for about 5,000 years.

10 Fun Things to See and Do in San Francisco

Here's Nate's list of things to see and do in San Francisco.

1. The **Golden Gate Bridge** is 1.7 miles long. You can drive (a limo), bike, or walk the span.

2. The **Exploratorium** is a funky museum. You can touch all of its more than 650 exhibits. Go to learn about science and have fun.

3. **Fisherman's Wharf** overlooks San Francisco Bay. Watch the fishing boats unload their catch.

4. **Sea Lions at Pier 39.** Stand on the pier. Watch and listen as the seals bark, nap, and swim.

5. San Francisco's **cable cars** are fancy trolleys. Underground cables pull the cars up steep hills. The cable cars are old. They've been running since 1873. Andrew Hallidie came up with the idea while watching horses pull the city's streetcars. He saw a team of five horses slip on a wet street. They slid backward down a steep hill. It was a terrible accident. Cables are safer in the hilly city.

6. Try climbing steep **Lombard Street**. It may be the most crooked street in the world. (Good place for a detective.)

7. Redwood trees grow in **Muir Woods**. These trees are huge! They grow as tall as thirty-six stories. They are old! Some live more than two centuries. Some of the movie *Return of the Jedi* was filmed in Muir Woods.

8. **Coit Tower** is 210 feet high. It was built in 1933. Lots of people say it looks like a fireman's hose. From the top, you get a great view of the city.

9. **Alcatraz Island (also known as the Rock)** was once a prison. It was famous for being hard to escape. To get away, you'd have to climb down a sheer cliff. Then you'd have to swim to San Francisco. The ocean water is cold. The tides are strong. Several prisoners got away. Everyone doubts they survived the swim. The prison closed in 1963. Now you can take a boat ride to the island. Pretend to lock yourself into a cell!

10. The **Japanese Tea Garden** is one neat thing to see in Golden Gate Park. Workers built it for the 1894 World's Fair.

How to Build
a Suspension Bridge

The Golden Gate is a suspension bridge. Steel and concrete make it strong. But suspension bridges aren't new. The Inca (South American Indians) built suspension bridges centuries ago. They used grass! Try building your own suspension bridge. See how strong you can make it.

GET TOGETHER:

- scissors
- several sheets of newspaper
- two chairs
- masking tape
- four paper clips
- a hole punch
- a foam cup
- coins

17

BUILD YOUR BRIDGE:

1. Cut the newspaper into strips. They can be as wide or narrow as you like. Make them at least two feet long.
2. Place the chairs about two feet apart. Connect the chairs with a "bridge" of newspaper. Use tape to secure the ends of the bridge.

3. Build a load tester to see how much weight your bridge can hold.
   - Unfold the paper clips into "S" shapes.
   - Punch three holes in the sides of the cup.
   - Slip a paper clip through each hole.
   - Hook a fourth paper clip through the other three clips. Now you have a hanger.
4. Hook your load tester to the bridge. Add coins to the cup until the bridge breaks.
5. Experiment to improve your bridge. Try twisting the newspaper. Or braid it. (TIP: Study pieces of twine or rope to see how they're made.)
6. How much weight can your strongest bridge carry?

San Francisco Jokes

Doctor, Doctor, I think I'm a bridge!
Why, what's come over you?
Two cars and a bus.

Doctor, Doctor, I think I'm a cable car!
Feeling strung out, are we?

Q: A penny and a quarter were rolling down the Golden Gate Bridge. Only the penny fell off. Why?
A: The quarter had more cents!

Knock, knock.
Who's there?
Cable cargo.
Cable cargo who?
Cable car go "clang clang."

Q: What did the prisoners at Alcatraz use to talk to each other?
A: Cell phones.

How to Make Joke Stew
(If You Want to Laugh)

Duncan got his jokes from a book. It was called Joke Stew. *What if he had made up his own jokes? Somebody's got to do it. Why don't you try?*

STEP ONE: Read a lot of jokes. Copy down the ones that make you laugh.

STEP TWO: Every joke has two parts. They are the **setup** and the **punch line.** The punch line is the funny ending.

Look at your list of funny jokes. Find each punch line. Think about what makes it funny. Is it silly? Or surprising? Or something else?

STEP THREE: Try writing a joke. Start with a simple one. Knock-knock jokes are easy. So are Doctor, Doctor jokes. (See page 20 for some examples.)

STEP FOUR: Try your jokes. Tell them to your mom. Any giggles? Try to make your best friend laugh. If you are shy, write your jokes down. Show them to someone you trust.

STEP FIVE: If your jokes flop, try rewriting them. Can you make them funnier?

STEP SIX: Don't give up! Jokes are hard to write. But it's worth the work. Everyone loves to laugh!

How to Make Joke Stew
(If You're Hungry)

No, this isn't really stew. It's Joke Stew. But it's still yummy!

GET TOGETHER:

- a bowl
- a spoon
- "meat"—a bowl of your favorite cereal
- "veggies"—a handful of fruit, like sliced banana, diced apples, blueberries, or dried cherries
- "spices"—a shake of cinnamon, nutmeg, or cocoa powder
- "broth"—milk

MAKE YOUR "STEW":

1. In the bowl, stir together the "meat,"
   "veggies," and "spices."
2. Add the "broth."
3. Eat!

Have you helped solve all Nate the Great's mysteries?

☐ **Nate the Great**: Meet Nate, the great detective, and join him as he uses incredible sleuthing skills to solve his first big case.

☐ **Nate the Great Goes Undercover**: Who— or what—is raiding Oliver's trash every night? Nate bravely hides out in his friend's garbage can to catch the smelly crook.

☐ **Nate the Great and the Lost List**: Nate loves pancakes, but who ever heard of cats eating them? Is a strange recipe at the heart of this mystery?

☐ **Nate the Great and the Phony Clue**: Against ferocious cats, hostile adversaries, and a sly phony clue, Nate struggles to prove that he's still the greatest detective.

☐ **Nate the Great and the Sticky Case**: Nate is stuck with his stickiest case yet as he hunts for his friend Claude's valuable stegosaurus stamp.

☐ **Nate the Great and the Missing Key**: Nate isn't afraid to look anywhere—even under the nose of his friend's ferocious dog, Fang—to solve the case of the missing key.

❑ **Nate the Great and the Snowy Trail**: Nate has his work cut out for him when his friend Rosamond loses the birthday present she was going to give him. How can he find the present when Rosamond won't even tell him what it is?

❑ **Nate the Great and the Fishy Prize**: The trophy for the Smartest Pet Contest has disappeared! Will Sludge, Nate's clue-sniffing dog, help solve the case and prove he's worthy of the prize?

❑ **Nate the Great Stalks Stupidweed**: When his friend Oliver loses his special plant, Nate searches high and low. Who knew a little weed could be so tricky?

❑ **Nate the Great and the Boring Beach Bag**: It's no relaxing day at the beach for Nate and his trusty dog, Sludge, as they search through sand and surf for signs of a missing beach bag.

❑ **Nate the Great Goes Down in the Dumps**: Nate discovers that the only way to clean up this case is to visit the town dump. Detective work can sure get dirty!

❑ **Nate the Great and the Halloween Hunt**: It's Halloween, but Nate isn't trick-or-treating for candy. Can any of the witches, pirates, and robots he meets help him find a missing cat?

❑ **Nate the Great and the Musical Note**: Nate is used to looking for clues, not listening for them! When he gets caught in the middle of a musical riddle, can he hear his way out?

❑ **Nate the Great and the Stolen Base**: It's not easy to track down a stolen base, and Nate's hunt leads him to some strange places before he finds himself at bat once more.

❑ **Nate the Great and the Pillowcase**: When a pillowcase goes missing, Nate must venture into the dead of night to search for clues. Everyone sleeps easier knowing Nate the Great is on the case!

❑ **Nate the Great and the Mushy Valentine**: Nate hates mushy stuff. But when someone leaves a big heart taped to Sludge's doghouse, Nate must help his favorite pooch discover his secret admirer.

❑ **Nate the Great and the Tardy Tortoise**: Where did the mysterious green tortoise in Nate's yard come from? Nate needs all his patience to follow this slow . . . slow . . . clue.

❑ **Nate the Great and the Crunchy Christmas**: It's Christmas, and Fang, Annie's scary dog, is not feeling jolly. Can Nate find Fang's crunchy Christmas mail before Fang crunches on *him*?

❑ **Nate the Great Saves the King of Sweden**: Can Nate solve his *first-ever* international case without leaving his own neighborhood?

❑ **Nate the Great and Me: The Case of the Fleeing Fang**: A surprise Happy Detective Day party is great fun for Nate until his friend's dog disappears! Help Nate track down the missing pooch, and learn all the tricks of the trade in a special fun section for aspiring detectives.

❑ **Nate the Great and the Monster Mess**: Nate loves his mother's deliciously spooky Monster Cookies, but the recipe has vanished! This is one case Nate and his growling stomach can't afford to lose.

❑ **Nate the Great, San Francisco Detective**: Nate visits his cousin Olivia Sharp in the big city, but it's no vacation. Can he find a lost joke book in time to save the world?

❑ **Nate the Great and the Big Sniff**: Nate depends on his dog, Sludge, to help him solve all his cases. But Nate is on his own this time, because Sludge has disappeared! Can Nate solve the case and recover his canine buddy?

❑ **Nate the Great on the Owl Express**: Nate boards a train to guard Hoot, his cousin Olivia Sharp's pet owl. Then Hoot vanishes! Can Nate find out *whooo* took the feathered creature?